This igloo book belongs to:

Dylan Hornstein

igloobooks

Published in 2017
by Igloo Books Ltd
Cottage Farm
Sywell
NN6 0BJ
www.igloobooks.com

REX001 0517
4 6 8 10 9 7 5 3
ISBN 978-1-78343-438-1

Written by Melanie Joyce
Illustrated by Gabrielle Murphy

Printed and manufactured in China

Love
makes the world
go round

igloobooks

Love is cuddling up when it's icy and cold.

Love is being **tickled** and **tumbled** and **rolled**.

Love is being **lost** and **finding** each other.

Love is my mom, dad, sister, and brother.

Love is the **best** present you've **ever** had.

Love is a **kiss** when you are feeling so **sad**.

Love is happiness. It's giving and sharing.

Love is tenderness, kindness, and caring.

Love makes the **world go round** and brings us together.

Love is about **friendships** that last forever.